PADDINGTON™

My Family and Friends

Written by Rebecca Adlard

Collins

Paddington is making a photo album.

This is the Brown family.

This is Judy.

This is Jonathan.

This is Mum.

This is Dad.

This is Mrs Bird.

This is Mr Gruber.

This is Aunt Lucy.

This is Paddington.

What a lot of family and friends.

What a lovely album!

Family and friends

Mum

family

Judy

Jonathan

Dad

Mrs Bird

Mr Gruber

Aunt Lucy

Paddington

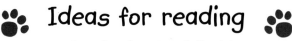# Ideas for reading

Written by Clare Dowdall, PhD
Lecturer and Primary Literacy Consultant

Reading objectives:
- read and understand simple sentences
- use phonic knowledge to decode regular words and read them aloud accurately
- read some common irregular words
- demonstrate understanding when talking with others about what they have read

Communication and language objectives:
- express themselves effectively, showing awareness of listeners' needs
- develop their own narratives and explanations by connecting ideas or events

Curriculum links: Personal social and emotional development – Managing feelings and behaviour; Making relationships; Literacy – Writing

Resources: photo album, digital camera, paper and pencils for writing letters

Word count: 61

Build a context for reading

- Read the title together. Ask children to think about who is in their family and who their special friends are (sensitivity about children's circumstances may be needed).
- Ask children to look carefully at the picture on the front cover. Help them to describe what they can see, and name any familiar characters from other Paddington books or the films.
- Read the blurb to the children: *Who are Paddington's family and friends?*

Understand and apply reading strategies

- Turn to pp2–3. Read the statements together: *Paddington is making a photo album. This is the Brown family.*
- Look at the words *photo album.* Help children to identify any known sounds and model how to read the words using phonic knowledge. Check that children know what a photo album is, and show them an example.
- Challenge children to look closely at the pictures on pp2–3. Can they find Paddington's camera? What do we know about the Brown family from their group photograph? Help children to use the pictures to make additional meaning.